Robert Louis Stevenson's

THE STRANGE CASE OF DR JEKYLL & MR HYDE

A retelling by
TANYA LANDMAN

Barrington Stoke

Published by Barrington Stoke
An imprint of HarperCollins*Publishers*
1 Robroyston Gate, Glasgow, G33 1JN

www.barringtonstoke.co.uk

HarperCollins*Publishers*
Macken House, 39/40 Mayor Street Upper,
Dublin 1, DO1 C9W8, Ireland

First published in 2026

Text © 2026 Tanya Landman
Cover illustration © 2026 Amy Blackwell
Cover design © 2026 HarperCollins*Publishers* Limited

The moral right of Tanya Landman to be identified
as the author of this work has been asserted in accordance
with the Copyright, Designs and Patents Act, 1988

ISBN 978-0-00-878910-7

10 9 8 7 6 5 4 3 2 1

All rights reserved. No part of this publication may be reproduced, stored in a retrieval system, or transmitted, in whole or in any part in any form or by any means, electronic, mechanical, photocopying, recording or otherwise without the prior permission in writing of the publisher and copyright owners

Without limiting the exclusive rights of any author, contributor or the publisher of this publication, any unauthorised use of this publication to train generative artificial intelligence (AI) technologies is expressly prohibited. HarperCollins also exercise their rights under Article 4(3) of the Digital Single Market Directive 2019/790 and expressly reserve this publication from the text and data mining exception

A catalogue record for this book is available from the British Library

Printed and bound in India by Replika Press Pvt. Ltd.

This book contains FSC™ certified paper and other controlled sources to ensure responsible forest management.

For more information visit: www.harpercollins.co.uk/green

*To the mighty and magnificent Mary,
with love and admiration*

CONTENTS

1. STORY OF THE DOOR — 1
2. SEARCH FOR MR HYDE — 8
3. DR JEKYLL WAS QUITE AT EASE — 16
4. THE CAREW MURDER CASE — 19
5. INCIDENT OF THE LETTER — 25
6. REMARKABLE INCIDENT OF DR LANYON — 32
7. INCIDENT AT THE WINDOW — 38
8. THE LAST NIGHT — 41
9. DR LANYON'S NARRATIVE — 54
10. HENRY JEKYLL'S FULL STATEMENT OF THE CASE — 60

1
STORY OF THE DOOR

Mr Utterson was a lawyer.

He was a long, lean, dull man who never smiled and was awkward in other people's company. Yet there was something loveable and very human about Mr Utterson. He was very strict with himself but had a great tolerance for other men's high spirits and the misdeeds that sometimes resulted from them. If a man chose a downward path towards disaster, Mr Utterson was often the last good and honest friend he could count on for help.

On Sundays, it was a habit of Mr Utterson's to stroll the streets of London with Mr Richard Enfield. Mr Enfield was Mr Utterson's distant relation and close friend.

On one of these rambles, the pair went down a clean and cheerful little street that shone out in contrast to its dingy neighbourhood like a fire in a forest. The houses and shops were freshly painted and polished. But two doors down from the corner was a passageway that led to a gloomy backyard. On the other side of it was a sinister block of a building that thrust itself onto the street. The whole place looked as if it had suffered years of neglect. It was two storeys high but had no windows. The only door had no knocker or bell, and its paint was peeling.

Mr Enfield pointed at it with his walking stick. "See that door?" he said to Mr Utterson. "I can tell you a very odd story about that."

"Really?" said Mr Utterson in a tight voice. "What's that?"

"I was walking home along here after a night out," Mr Enfield began. "It was about three in the morning. The place was deserted. Everyone was fast asleep, but street after street was all lit up as if a carnival parade was about to begin. And then I saw two figures – a small man walking very fast and a little girl running from the opposite direction. Not surprisingly, the two crashed into each other at the corner. But then came the horrible part: the man trampled calmly over the girl's body and left her screaming on the ground. It sounds like nothing, but it was hellish to see. The man didn't seem human, but like some damned juggernaut, an unstoppable machine.

"I ran after him and brought him back. The girl's family had heard her screams, so by then there was a group of very angry people gathered around her. Yet the man was perfectly cool and calm. He didn't put up any resistance when I got him but gave me a look so ugly it made me drip with sweat.

"It turned out the girl had been sent to fetch a doctor, and then he arrived as well. The doctor examined her and said she was not much hurt, and you'd think that would have been the end of it. But it was very odd. I had taken a dislike to that small man at first sight, as had the girl's family.

"That seemed natural. What struck me was the doctor's reaction to him. He was a dry, dour Scottish man. You know the type – normally about as emotional as a bagpipe. Yet that doctor had turned white with a desire to kill the small man. I knew what was in the doctor's mind just as he knew what was in mine. But as killing was out of the question, we did the next best thing. We told the man that if he did not put things right, we would make such a scandal that his name would stink from one end of London to the other. If he had any friends, he would lose them.

"All the time we were talking to the small man, we had to keep the girl's mother and aunts and sisters from attacking him. They were as wild as harpies. I never saw such a circle of faces filled with hate! And the man at the middle of it all simply stared back at us and sneered as if he were the devil himself.

"'If you choose to make capital out of this accident by blackmailing me,' said he, 'I am naturally helpless. Every gentleman wishes to avoid a scandal. Name your price.'

"In the end, we agreed the small man would give a hundred pounds to the girl's family as compensation. He went off to fetch the money, and the doctor and I followed him. Where do you think he went? Straight to that door in the sinister building. He whipped out a key, went in and came back with ten pounds in cash and a cheque for ninety pounds.

"That cheque was not signed by him. I won't tell you whose name was on it, but it was a very well-known and very respectable gentleman. I assumed the cheque was a fake, but the man swore it was not. He declared that he would stay with me until the banks were open, cash the cheque himself and hand the money over.

"So we all set off together to my house – the doctor, the child's father, the small man and myself. We spent the remainder of the night there. After we had breakfasted, off we all went to the bank. I handed the cheque to the clerk and told him I thought it was a fake. But no. That cheque was real."

"Ah," said Mr Utterson.

"It's a bad story, isn't it?" Mr Enfield sighed. "The man who trampled down that poor child was a damnable creature. The person who signed that cheque for him is a perfect gentleman, so it must be that he is being blackmailed. Paying the price for some youthful indiscretion. Blackmail House is what I call that place with the door now."

A silence fell over the two men until Mr Utterson asked, "The man who signed the cheque, does he live in that building?"

"No," said Mr Enfield.

"And have you ever asked anyone about it?" said Mr Utterson.

"No! If I started asking questions, it'd be like starting a stone rolling down a hill. It sets off other stones, and before you know it, some old bird gets knocked on the head in his own back garden and there's such a scandal the whole family have to change their name. No, I make it a rule that the shadier things look, the less I ask about them."

"A very good rule," said Mr Utterson. It was one he mostly followed himself.

"However, I have noticed some things about the place," Mr Enfield said. "There's only that one door, and the only person who goes in or out is the damnable man I met that night. There are three windows on the first floor that look out over the backyard but no windows on the ground floor. There's a chimney, and smoke comes out, so someone must live there. But I can't be sure who – the buildings here are so packed together it's hard to tell where one ends and another begins."

The pair walked on in silence.

And then Mr Utterson said, "Your rule not to ask questions is a good one, Enfield. But I want to ask the name of the man who walked over the child."

"Well ..." said Mr Enfield. "I can't see what harm that would do. It was a man by the name of Hyde."

"What does he look like?" asked Mr Utterson.

"He is not easy to describe. There is something wrong with his appearance, something displeasing, something downright detestable. I never saw a man I so disliked, yet I don't know why. He must be deformed somewhere – he gives off that feeling. Yet I can't tell you how or where!"

Again, the men walked in silence, and then Mr Utterson asked, "You're sure he had a key?"

"My dear sir ..." Mr Enfield protested.

"I know my curiosity seems strange," said Mr Utterson. "But the fact is, I didn't ask you the name of the man who wrote that cheque, as I already know who he is ... So if you have been inexact at any point in your story, please correct it."

"I have been exact in every detail!" Mr Enfield replied a little crossly. "Hyde had a key and still does. I saw him use it only a week ago."

Mr Utterson sighed very deeply but said nothing more.

When they finished their walk, both men agreed to never discuss the matter again. They shook hands on it and parted.

2
SEARCH FOR MR HYDE

Mr Utterson returned home feeling unsettled and ate his dinner without relish. On a Sunday evening, he often sat by the fire and read some dry, religious book until midnight. Then he would go to bed grateful and sober.

But on that Sunday evening, Mr Utterson went to his study after he had eaten, opened his safe and took out an envelope marked "Dr Jekyll's Will".

It was an odd document that had long troubled Mr Utterson. He was Jekyll's old friend and lawyer, but he'd had no part in shaping the will. Henry Jekyll had written it himself and placed it into Utterson's hands to be acted upon when the time came. The will declared that on the death of Henry Jekyll, all his possessions were to go to "his friend Edward Hyde". It also said that if Dr Jekyll disappeared for three months or more,

Edward Hyde should step into Henry Jekyll's shoes without delay.

Dr Jekyll's will upset Mr Utterson both as a lawyer and as a man of sense. Before today, he'd had no idea who Mr Hyde was, and that had worried him. Now that he knew a little bit about the man, it worried him even more.

Mr Utterson had thought Jekyll was afflicted with madness when he wrote his will. Now he feared Jekyll was being blackmailed and threatened with deep, dark disgrace.

Mr Utterson put on a coat and set off towards Cavendish Square, where his friend Dr Lanyon lived and worked.

If anyone knows about this business, it will be Lanyon, he thought.

Mr Utterson arrived at Lanyon's house, and the butler showed him to the dining room. Dr Lanyon sat there alone with his wine. Lanyon was a hearty, red-faced gentleman who sprang up from his chair and welcomed Utterson in with both hands. The two old friends had been at school and college together and had always greatly enjoyed each other's company. After a little idle chatter, Utterson introduced the subject that was bothering him.

"I suppose," he said, "that you and I are the two oldest friends that Henry Jekyll has?"

Lanyon agreed but added, "I see little of him now."

"Really?" said Utterson. "I thought you were bonded by your mutual interest in science?"

"We were," replied Lanyon. "But Henry Jekyll's ideas became too fanciful for me more than ten years ago. He began to go wrong in his mind. Spouted such unscientific rubbish!" Lanyon's face flushed an angry purple at the very thought. "It was too much for even the strongest of friendships to endure."

Mr Utterson did not pursue the matter. Instead, he asked, "Did you ever come across a friend of his – a man called Hyde?"

Lanyon had never heard of him, and so Utterson returned to his home and his bed. There he tossed and turned until the small hours of the morning began to grow large. First, Utterson was haunted by dreams of a man walking swiftly, a child running, a human juggernaut mowing her down and passing on despite her screams.

But then Utterson dreamed of a bedroom in a splendid house where Jekyll lay asleep in a four-poster bed. Its curtains were being pulled back, and Jekyll was being woken by a small man whose face and features Utterson could not see. He was then forced to do the small man's bidding ...

In the morning, Utterson knew he needed to see Hyde in the flesh. He thought that if he could set eyes on the man, he might find the reason Jekyll had written his will in that odd way. If he could discover why his old friend Jekyll had such an interest in Hyde, it might put his mind at rest.

And so Mr Utterson lingered about the sinister building and the shabby door – in the morning before office hours, at noon when the place was busy, and at night under the fogged city moon.

If he be Mr Hyde, he thought, *I shall be Mr Seek*.

It was a fine, dry night with frost in the air when Mr Utterson's patience was rewarded. The street was lonely and silent. Small sounds carried far. Standing in the shadows, Mr Utterson heard an odd, light footstep drawing near. At last, a small man, plainly dressed, came around the corner. Even at a distance, there was something repulsive about him. The man pulled a key from his pocket and made straight for the door.

Mr Utterson stepped out and touched him on the shoulder. "Mr Hyde?" he asked.

Mr Hyde shrank back with a hissing intake of breath, replying, "What do you want?"

"I'm Mr Utterson – an old friend of Dr Jekyll's. You must have heard my name. Will you let me in?"

"Dr Jekyll is not at home," Mr Hyde said and turned to go.

Mr Utterson said quickly, "Do me a favour. Will you let me see your face?"

Mr Hyde hesitated but then turned with a defiant air. The two men stared at each other for a few seconds.

"Now I shall recognise you if I see you again," said Mr Utterson. "It may be useful."

"Yes," agreed Mr Hyde. "It's good that we have met. And you should know my address." He gave Mr Utterson the house number of a very disreputable street in Soho.

Good God! thought Mr Utterson. *Is he thinking of the will too?* But he kept his feelings to himself.

"How did you know who I am?" demanded Mr Hyde.

"You were described to me," replied Mr Utterson. "We have friends in common. Jekyll, for example."

"Lies! He never told you about me!" cried Mr Hyde with a flush of anger. "I didn't think a man like you would lie."

"That is not fitting language!" protested Mr Utterson.

At that, Hyde gave a snarl that turned into a savage laugh. Then, with extraordinary speed, he unlocked the door and vanished inside.

For a while, Mr Utterson stood unmoving but then turned and began to walk along the street, utterly confused. Mr Hyde was pale and dwarfish, giving an impression of deformity without any nameable malformation. There was something wrong with him, some part that was badly made, yet Mr Utterson couldn't think what!

Hyde had an evil smile and seemed to be a murderous mix of timidity and boldness. He spoke with a husky, broken voice. But not even all these things together could explain the disgust, loathing and fear that Utterson had felt when looking at Hyde. He had never experienced anything like it!

"The man seems hardly human!" he muttered to himself. "What foul soul is contained within that body? Oh, my poor Henry Jekyll, your new friend has the face of the Devil!"

Mr Utterson walked around the corner into a square of what had once been handsome houses. Most had now been turned into small flats and shady offices. The only house that remained undivided belonged to Henry Jekyll. It wore its old air of wealth and comfort. When Mr Utterson knocked on its front door, the elderly butler named Poole let him in.

Mr Utterson warmed himself by the fire while Poole went in search of his master. Utterson had always thought Jekyll's house to be the most pleasant place in London, but tonight he felt a shudder in his blood and a gloom in his spirits. There seemed to be a menace in the flickering firelight and the shadows that jumped across the ceiling. It was a relief when Poole returned to announce that Dr Jekyll had gone out.

"I saw Mr Hyde go in the old dissecting-room door, Poole," Mr Utterson said. "Is that all right when Dr Jekyll is away from home?"

"Quite all right, Mr Utterson sir," replied the servant. "Mr Hyde has a key."

"Your master seems to put a great deal of trust in that young man."

"Yes, sir, he does indeed," said Poole. "We all have orders to obey him."

"I don't think I've ever met Mr Hyde here?" asked Mr Utterson.

"Oh dear no, sir. He never dines here," replied the butler. "We see very little of him on this side of the house. He comes and goes through the back way."

There was nothing more to be said. Mr Utterson returned to his own home with a very heavy heart.

Poor Jekyll! he thought. *I fear he is in deep water. Well, he was wild when he was young. And now the ghost of some old, long-buried sin, the cancer of some concealed disgrace has been dug up and is being used against him.*

A spark of hope flashed in the lawyer's mind. *But Mr Hyde must surely have secrets of his own!* Utterson thought. *Dark secrets, by the look of him. Things cannot go on as they are. If Hyde knows about the will, he might grow impatient to inherit! I will get to work on this, if Jekyll will only let me ...*

3
DR JEKYLL WAS QUITE AT EASE

A fortnight later, Dr Jekyll invited a few old friends for dinner, including Mr Utterson. They were all intelligent, reputable men and all fond of good wine, so the evening was a very pleasant one. After the other guests had left, Mr Utterson lingered behind. This was nothing new. People who liked Mr Utterson liked him very much indeed. Hosts often detained the lawyer after their loud, laughing guests had departed to sit for a while in Utterson's rich, restful silence.

Dr Jekyll was a large, handsome, smooth-faced man of fifty. There was perhaps something a little sly about him, but he was also capable and kind. He had a warm and sincere affection for Mr Utterson.

The two men sat quietly by the fire until Utterson said, "I have been wanting to speak to you about that will of yours …"

A close observer might have noticed that the topic brought Jekyll pain. However, he replied cheerfully, "Poor Utterson! I never saw a man as upset as you were by my will. You looked just like Lanyon when he objected to my so-called scientific heresies! Oh, I know Lanyon's a good fellow, but he's also a pedant. An ignorant, blatant pedant. I was never more disappointed in any man than Lanyon."

Mr Utterson ignored this new topic and pursued the subject of the will. "I never approved of it," he said. "And now that I have learned something of Hyde—"

Dr Jekyll's face paled. "I thought we'd agreed to let the matter drop long ago. You don't understand. I'm in a strange and difficult position. It can't be helped by talking."

"Jekyll," said Utterson. "You know me. I'm a man to be trusted. Tell me what the trouble is. I am sure I can get you out of it."

"It is good of you," replied the doctor. "I trust you more than any man alive, but it isn't what you imagine. It's not as bad as that. I can be rid of Mr Hyde whenever I choose. I give you my word on that. I thank you again and again, but this is a private matter, Utterson. I beg you to let it rest."

Utterson sat looking at the fire. "Very well," he said at last, getting to his feet.

"There is one thing I want you to understand," said Jekyll. "I know you've seen Hyde: he told me so, and I am sorry if he was rude. But I do sincerely take a very great interest in that young man. If anything happens to me, I want you to promise that you will stand by him and get him his rights. It would be a great weight off my mind if you would promise me that."

"I shall never like him," said the lawyer.

"I don't ask you to." Jekyll laid a hand on his friend's arm. "I ask only for justice. I only ask you to help him for my sake when I am no longer here."

Utterson heaved a sigh. "I promise."

4
THE CAREW MURDER CASE

A year later, London was shocked by a brutal crime. It was made all the more newsworthy because of the victim's high position in society.

A maid servant who lived alone in a house not far from the river had gone upstairs to bed at about 11 p.m. A fog rolled over the city a few hours later, but that early part of the night was cloudless. The lane that the maid's window overlooked was brilliantly lit by the full moon. She had a romantic nature, and as she sat down to look out of the window, she fell into a daydream.

As she watched, an old and beautiful gentleman with white hair came along the lane. A small man was coming from the other direction, a walking stick in his hand. The old gentleman bowed and greeted the other and appeared to be asking the way. The moon shone on his face, and the maid thought the old man seemed kind and gracious.

Her eye then wandered to the small man, and she recognised Mr Hyde. He had visited her master once, and the maid had taken an instant dislike to him. Mr Hyde didn't reply to the old man's question. Suddenly, he stamped his foot angrily and waved his walking stick like a madman.

The old gentleman stepped back, very much surprised. And at that, Mr Hyde lost all control. He clubbed the old gentleman to the ground and then trampled his victim underfoot with ape-like fury. He hailed down a storm of blows, and the old man's bones audibly shattered. The maid fainted with horror.

It was 2 a.m. before she revived and called the police. By then, the murderer was long gone, but his mangled victim still lay in the middle of the lane. The attack was so savage that the killer's walking stick had broken in two. One half had been carried away by the murderer, but the other had rolled into the gutter. The victim's pockets contained a purse and a gold watch, but there were no cards or papers to identify him. There was nothing but a sealed, stamped envelope that the victim had probably been on his way to post. It was addressed to Mr Utterson and was therefore taken to the lawyer before he was even out of bed.

"I shall say nothing until I have seen the body," Mr Utterson said when he learned the details of the attack. "This may be very serious." After he had dressed and breakfasted, he went to the police station, where he identified the murdered man as Sir Danvers Carew.

"Good God, sir," exclaimed the police inspector. His eyes lit up with professional ambition. "This will be a sensation," he muttered to himself. And then he added to Mr Utterson, "Perhaps you can help us find the culprit."

Inspector Newcomen explained everything the maid had seen and showed Mr Utterson the half of the broken walking stick. It was one that Mr Utterson had given to Henry Jekyll many years before.

"Did the maid say Mr Hyde was a small man?" he asked.

"She said he was very small and very wicked looking," replied the inspector.

Mr Utterson paused a moment. Then, raising his head, he said, "I can take you to Mr Hyde's house."

It was about 9 a.m., and the first fog of the season had rolled in. Clouds the colour of chocolate hung over the city as the cab carrying Mr Utterson and the police inspector crawled from street to street.

Lamps had been lit to combat this mournful re-invasion of darkness. To Utterson, Soho seemed like a district of some city in a nightmare. As the cab drew up, the fog lifted a little to reveal a dingy street. Ragged children huddled in doorways, and women slipped out to have a morning glass at the gin-palace on the corner. This was the street where Henry Jekyll's heir chose to live.

A silver-haired housekeeper opened the door. She said that this was Mr Hyde's house, but he was not at home. He had been in and gone out again an hour later. But then Mr Hyde was often away, she told them. She hadn't seen him for two months until he showed up yesterday. When Mr Utterson asked to see inside the house, the woman declared it was impossible. So he added, "This is Inspector Newcomen of Scotland Yard."

The housekeeper's face lit up with wicked joy. "He is in trouble!" she said. "What has he done?"

"My good woman," the inspector said, "just let me and this gentleman have a look about."

There was little to see. It was a large house but mostly empty. Mr Hyde had only used two rooms, which were furnished with luxurious good taste. A cupboard was filled with good wine, the tableware was silver, the cloth and napkins were fine linen. A beautiful oil painting hung on the wall. Mr Utterson supposed it had been a gift from Henry Jekyll, who was a keen art collector.

The place looked as if it had been ransacked. Clothes lay about the floor, drawers stood open, and in the fireplace a pile of ashes showed that many documents and letters had recently been burned. The inspector raked the remains of a cheque book from the embers. He was delighted when he then found the other half of the walking stick behind the door.

After leaving the house, the two men visited the bank. Mr Hyde had an account that was thousands of pounds in credit.

"He must have panicked or he'd never have left the stick or burned the cheque book," Inspector Newcomen said with glee. "Money's life to the man. All we have to do is wait for him at the bank and get out the handcuffs."

But capturing Hyde was not as easy as the inspector hoped. Hyde did not visit the bank that morning, and there seemed nowhere obvious to look for him. Hyde had no friends or family. Even the maid servant's master had only seen him twice.

Hyde had never been photographed. The few people who could describe him agreed on only one detail: the haunting sense of deformity that overwhelmed anyone who met him.

5
INCIDENT OF THE LETTER

Late that afternoon, Mr Utterson arrived at Dr Jekyll's house. Poole let him in. The lawyer followed the butler down the stairs, into the kitchen and across a yard to the shabby building that had once been a dissecting room. Dr Jekyll had bought the house from a surgeon, but his own interests were more chemical than anatomical, and he had changed the place into a laboratory.

It was the first time Mr Utterson had entered the building, and he eyed it with both curiosity and distaste. The windowless ground floor had once been a theatre where eager medical students had watched surgeons dissecting dead bodies. It was now silent and muddled, the tables covered in chemical apparatus, the floor strewn with crates and littered with packing straw. At the far end, a flight of stairs led to a door covered with red baize fabric. When Poole opened it, Mr Utterson entered Dr Jekyll's study.

It was large, fitted all round with glass-fronted cabinets. A tilting full-length mirror stood beside a desk. The three dusty windows that looked out into the yard were barred with iron. A fire burned in the grate and a lamp was lit, for the fog was lying thickly even in here.

Huddled close to the fire sat Dr Jekyll. He looked deadly sick. He did not get up to meet his visitor but simply held out a cold hand and welcomed him in a weak voice.

"You've heard the news?" said Mr Utterson as soon as Poole had left them.

The doctor shuddered. "Yes. The newspaper sellers were shouting it in the square."

"Carew was my client, but so are you," said Utterson. "I want to know what I am caught up in. You have not been mad enough to hide his murderer?"

"Utterson, I swear to God," the doctor cried. "I will never set eyes on him again. I am done with Hyde. It is at an end. He does not even want my help. He is safe. Mark my words, he will never be heard of again."

The lawyer listened gloomily, for he did not like Jekyll's feverish manner. "You seem very sure of it. I hope you're right. If it came to a trial, your name might be dragged into this."

"I am sure of it," replied Jekyll. "I cannot tell you why, but I am certain. However, there is one thing you can advise me on. I have received a letter, and I don't know if I should show it to the police. I would like to leave it with you, Utterson. You will judge wisely, I am sure."

"You fear it might lead to Hyde's capture?" asked the lawyer.

"I don't care what becomes of Hyde! I was thinking of my own reputation. This hateful business has left me rather exposed."

Utterson was both surprised and relieved by his friend's selfishness. "Let me see the letter," he said.

It was in oddly upright handwriting and signed "Edward Hyde". In it, Hyde said that he had repaid Jekyll's generosity very badly. He told Jekyll not to be afraid, because he had a sure and certain means of escape.

"Do you have the envelope?" Mr Utterson asked.

"I burned it," replied Jekyll. "But there was no postmark. It was delivered by hand."

"Shall I keep this and sleep on it?" asked Utterson.

"I will leave it to you," Jekyll replied. "I have lost all confidence in myself."

The lawyer then said, "One more thing. Was it Hyde who dictated the terms in your will about your disappearance?"

The doctor looked faint. He shut his mouth tight and nodded.

"I knew it," said Utterson. "Hyde meant to murder you. You've had a lucky escape."

"I've had something far more useful," said the doctor solemnly. "I've had a lesson. Oh God, Utterson, what a lesson I've had!" Jekyll covered his face with his hands.

Mr Utterson left Dr Jekyll alone then, but on his way out of the house he stopped to ask Poole who had delivered the letter. Poole replied that nothing had arrived by hand that day. All Utterson's fears were renewed. Perhaps the letter had been delivered to the laboratory's back door? Or was it possible that Hyde had actually written it there?

He walked along the street. The cries of newspaper sellers rang in his ears: "Special edition! Shocking murder!"

Sir Danvers Carew had been a friend and client of Utterson's. It seemed that the good name of Dr Jekyll, another friend and client, would be sucked into the scandal. Utterson was used to relying on himself, but he suddenly longed for some sensible advice. And so, when he got home, he sat down by the fire to share a bottle of wine with his head clerk – a man named Mr Guest.

The fog still slept on the wing above the drowned city, where lamps glimmered like carbuncles. But the firelight was bright, and the wine brought a warm glow of hot afternoons on hillside vineyards into the room and seemed to set free and disperse the fogs of London.

The lawyer melted. There was no one from who Utterson kept fewer secrets than Mr Guest. In fact, he was not sure he kept any. Mr Guest had often been on business to Dr Jekyll's. He knew Poole and could not have failed to know about Hyde's visits to the house. Mr Guest also knew a great deal about handwriting and was a man of very sound judgement. It seemed sensible for Utterson to show his clerk the letter. Mr Guest would surely make some wise remark or other. And then Utterson would know what course of future action he should take.

"This is a sad business about Sir Danvers," Utterson began.

"Yes, sir," the clerk agreed. "The murderer must have been a madman!"

"I'd like to hear your views on that," replied Utterson. "I have something he has written here."

He handed the letter over.

When Mr Guest had studied it, he said, "No ... the man who penned this was not mad. But it is very odd handwriting."

"And a very odd writer!" said the lawyer.

Just then, a servant entered with a note for Mr Utterson.

"Is that from Dr Jekyll, sir?" asked Mr Guest. Mr Utterson nodded, and he continued, "I thought I knew the writing. Is it private, Mr Utterson?"

"Only an invitation to dinner. Why? Do you want to see it?"

"Yes, sir. Thank you." The clerk laid Jekyll's dinner invitation alongside Hyde's note and compared them. "Interesting ..."

There was a pause, then Mr Guest added, "There's a great similarity. The handwriting in both is pretty much identical – they just slope in different directions."

"Rather odd," said Utterson very carefully.

"It is, as you say, rather odd," nodded Mr Guest.

Another pause.

"I wouldn't speak to anyone about this," said the master.

"No, sir," said the clerk. "I understand."

As soon as Utterson was alone, he locked the letter in his safe. He was deeply shocked. Henry Jekyll had forged the letter for a murderer! The very thought made the blood run cold in his veins.

6
REMARKABLE INCIDENT OF DR LANYON

Time passed. The public were outraged by the savage murder of Sir Danvers. Thousands of pounds were offered in reward for Edward Hyde's capture. But the man had disappeared as if he had never existed. Many tales came out about his cruelty, his vile, violent past life and his many misdeeds. But there was not a whisper about his present whereabouts. Hyde had left his house in Soho on the morning of the murder and simply vanished.

Gradually, Mr Utterson's heated panic faded, and he became more calm. He thought that the death of Sir Danvers was more than paid for by the disappearance of Mr Hyde. Now that Hyde's evil influence had been withdrawn, a new life had begun for Jekyll. The doctor renewed old friendships, did good work for charities, attended church. He was busy, out in the open air, and his face seemed brighter and more open. For more than two months, Dr Jekyll was peaceful and content.

On January 8th, Utterson had dined at the doctor's. Lanyon had been there, and it was as it had been in the old days when the three of them were close friends. But on the 12th, and again on the 14th, Jekyll's door was shut against the lawyer. Poole informed Utterson that Jekyll was confined to the house and seeing no one.

On the 15th, Utterson tried again and was again refused. For two months, he had grown used to seeing his friend almost every day. Jekyll's return to solitude weighed heavily on Utterson. On the fifth night of it, he invited Mr Guest to dine with him. On the sixth, he took himself off to Dr Lanyon's.

At Lanyon's, the door was not shut against Utterson. But when he entered, he was shocked by the sudden change in Lanyon's appearance. The rosy-faced man was pale, his ample flesh had melted away; he looked close to death. But worse than his physical decline was a look in Lanyon's eye that suggested he was in the grip of terror.

Utterson assumed that Lanyon knew he was close to death and was terrified, but when he remarked on his friend's sickly looks, Lanyon calmly declared he was a doomed man.

"I've had a shock and shall never recover," he said. "It is only a matter of weeks. Well, life has been pleasant. I liked it. I *used* to like it. I sometimes think if we knew everything, we would all be more glad to get away."

"Jekyll is ill too," said Utterson. "Have you seen him?"

Lanyon held up a trembling hand. "I wish to see or hear no more of Dr Jekyll," he said in a loud, unsteady voice. "I am done with him. I regard him as dead."

After a long pause, Mr Utterson said gently, "Can't I do anything? We three are very old friends. We shall not live to make others."

"Nothing can be done," said Lanyon. "Ask him."

"He won't see me," said the lawyer.

"I'm not surprised," Lanyon replied. "Some day, after I'm dead, you may come to learn the rights and wrongs of this. But I can't tell you now. Talk of other things. And if you can't keep off this accursed topic, then go. I cannot bear it."

As soon as Utterson got home, he wrote to Jekyll asking why he was excluded from the house and what was the cause of the unhappy break with Lanyon. The following day, an answer came, pathetically worded and darkly mysterious in its tone.

The quarrel with Lanyon was incurable, Jekyll wrote. "I don't blame our old friend, but I share his view that we must never meet. I mean to lead a life of extreme seclusion from now on. Do not be surprised, do not doubt my friendship if my door is shut to you. You must allow me to go my own dark way. I have brought on myself a punishment and a danger that I cannot name. I am the chief of sinners, but I am also the chief of sufferers. You can do only one thing, Utterson: respect my silence."

Utterson was amazed. Hyde had vanished, Jekyll had been his old self, and only a week ago there was every promise of him enjoying a cheerful, honourable old age. In a single moment, everything had somehow been wrecked.

A week later, Lanyon took to his bed. In less than a fortnight, he was dead. The night after the funeral, a letter arrived for Utterson. The lawyer locked himself into his study. In the light of one melancholy candle, he read:

*Private: for the hands of G.J. Utterson
alone, and if he should die before me, to
be destroyed unread.*

It was Lanyon's handwriting. Utterson opened it, but inside was another envelope, also sealed and with the instruction:

*Not to be opened until the death or
disappearance of Dr Henry Jekyll.*

The words "death" and "disappearance" together again, just as they had been in Jekyll's mad will! Written by Lanyon – what did it mean?

Curiosity overwhelmed Utterson. He longed to ignore the instruction, open the envelope and get to the bottom of this mystery. But professional honour and loyalty to his dead friend held him back. He placed the envelope in his safe.

From that moment, Utterson's thoughts about Jekyll were uneasy and fearful. He still felt kindly towards him and still called at the house but was perhaps relieved to be denied entry every time. Jekyll had imprisoned himself and become a recluse. Utterson preferred to speak with Poole on the doorstep in the open air, with the sounds of the city all about them.

The butler only ever had bad news. Dr Jekyll had confined himself to his study, Poole said. Dr Jekyll was out of spirits, as if something weighed heavily on his mind. Day followed day and Jekyll's condition never changed. Utterson called less and less often.

7
INCIDENT AT THE WINDOW

One Sunday, Mr Utterson took his usual walk with Mr Enfield. Once more, the pair went down the clean and cheerful little street. They reached the sinister building with the shabby door and stopped to gaze at it.

"Well," said Enfield, "that story is at an end. We shall never see Mr Hyde again."

"I hope not," said Utterson.

"You must have thought me very ignorant, not knowing this was the back way to Dr Jekyll's!"

"You found out, did you?" said Utterson. "Well, if you know that, we may as well go into the yard and take a look up at the windows. I'm worried about Jekyll. A friend's presence might do him good."

The sky overhead was bright, yet the yard was cool and damp and dark. Looking up, they saw that one of the three barred windows was half open. Dr Jekyll was sitting sadly by it, like a prisoner.

"Jekyll!" Utterson called. "Are you any better?"

"I am very low, Utterson," replied the doctor dully.

"You stay indoors too much," said the lawyer. "You should be out taking exercise like Mr Enfield and me." He introduced the two men to each other and then added, "Come now – get your hat. Take a short walk with us."

"You are very kind," sighed Jekyll. "I should like to very much ... but no, no, no, it is impossible. I dare not. But I am very glad to see you, Utterson. It really is a great pleasure. I would ask you in, but the place is not fit to be seen."

"Then we will stay and speak with you from here," said the lawyer.

"I was about to suggest that!" Jekyll replied with a smile. But as soon as the words were out of his mouth, his smile vanished. His face became a picture of such pure terror and despair that it froze the blood of the gentlemen below.

It was just for a second. Then the window was thrust down, and they saw Jekyll no more. But they'd only needed one glimpse. They left without a word and walked along the little street. It was not until they came to the main road that Mr Utterson turned and looked at his companion. Each man saw his own horror reflected in the other's eyes. Both were as pale as death.

"God forgive us, God forgive us," said Mr Utterson.

Mr Enfield nodded his head very seriously, and the men walked on once more in silence.

8
THE LAST NIGHT

Mr Utterson was sitting at his fireside one evening when Dr Jekyll's butler, Poole, came to see him.

"What brings you here?" asked Utterson, very much surprised. He took a closer look at Poole's worried face and asked, "What ails you? Is the doctor ill?"

"Mr Utterson," said the butler, "there is something wrong."

"Take a seat," Utterson said. "Here's a glass of wine for you. Take your time."

Poole said at last, "The doctor's shut himself up again. I don't like it, sir. I'm afraid. I've been afraid a week, and I can't bear it any more."

Poole looked terrible. He sat with the wine untasted, staring at the floor. "I think there's been foul play."

"Foul play?" cried the lawyer. He was frightened and therefore irritable. "Whatever do you mean?"

"Will you come with me and see for yourself?" asked Poole.

Mr Utterson's only answer was to put on his coat and hat and follow the butler out into the street.

It was a wild, cold night in March, with a pale moon lying on her back as if the wind had blown her over. Thin clouds were shredded across the sky. The square was a whirlwind of dust. Trees lashed themselves against the railings.

Poole had walked a pace or two ahead of Utterson all the way. Now he stopped suddenly, took off his hat and mopped his brow with a red handkerchief. His face was white. When he spoke, his voice was cracked and broken.

"Well, sir," Poole said. "Here we are. God grant there be nothing wrong."

Utterson nodded and replied, "Amen to that, Poole."

Poole knocked on Jekyll's front door, and it opened just a crack, still on the chain. A voice asked, "Is that you, Poole?"

"Yes," said Poole. "Open the door."

Inside, the hall was brightly lit with a fire built high. All the servants stood huddled together by it like a flock of sheep. At the sight of Mr Utterson, one of the housemaids burst into tears, and the cook ran forward as if to embrace him.

"What are you all doing here?" Utterson said crossly. "This is very irregular. Very unseemly. Your master would be far from pleased."

"They're all afraid," said Poole.

A silence followed that was broken only by the maid's weeping.

"Hold your tongue!" Poole snapped, showing his own jangled nerves. Taking a candle, he begged Mr Utterson to follow him, and the pair went down the stairs, into the kitchen and across the yard.

"Come as quietly as you can," Poole said when they reached the laboratory. "I want you to hear but not be heard. And if by any chance he asks you in, don't go."

Mr Utterson's nerves jerked, nearly throwing him off balance, but he followed the butler into the building. They walked through the surgical theatre to the stairs. Here, Poole signalled to Utterson to stand and listen while he knocked on the red baize door of the study with a shaking hand.

"Mr Utterson has arrived at the house, sir. He's asking to see you," Poole called.

A voice from within answered, "Tell him I can't see anyone."

"Very good, sir," Poole replied. Silently, he then led Mr Utterson back across the yard and into the kitchen, where the fire was out and beetles scuttled across the floor.

"Was that my master's voice?" Poole asked Mr Utterson.

"It seems much changed," the lawyer replied, very pale.

"Changed? Yes! I've been twenty years in this house – I know his voice! That's not him! My master's been got rid of. He was got rid of eight days ago when we heard him crying out in the name of God. And who's in there instead of him and why it stays there is a thing that cries to Heaven, Mr Utterson!"

"This is a very wild, strange tale, Poole," said Mr Utterson, biting his finger nervously. "Suppose it is what you think? Suppose Dr Jekyll has been ... murdered – why on earth would his killer stay? It doesn't make sense."

"You're a hard man to satisfy, Mr Utterson, but I'll do it," said Poole. "All last week, whatever's in there was crying out night and day for some sort of medicine. Whenever the master was working, he used to write his orders for chemicals on a piece of paper and throw it onto the stairs for me to take to his supplier. There's been nothing but orders this week, written on paper, two or three times a day. I've been sent running to every chemist in London. But no sooner do I bring the stuff back than there's another piece of paper telling me to return it because it's no good. Then there's another order to a different chemist. The drug is wanted bitter bad, sir."

"Have you any of these papers?" asked Mr Utterson.

Poole pulled a crumpled note from his pocket, and the lawyer examined it.

It was addressed to a chemist and complained that the last sample they had sent was impure and useless. It went on:

> *Dr Jekyll purchased a large quantity some years ago and now begs them to search with care. If any of the same quality is left, send it to him at once. Expense is no matter. The importance of this to Dr J. cannot be exaggerated.*

The note looked reasonable until the end, when the writer's emotion had broken loose. A sudden splutter of the pen and he had scrawled: "For God's sake, find me some of the old."

"A strange note," said Mr Utterson. "It is the doctor's handwriting, isn't it?"

"It looks like it," said Poole. "But what does that matter? I've seen the thing that's in there! I came in when it slipped out and was digging among all the crates, looking for the drug. It whipped up the stairs at once, so I only got a glimpse, but my hair stood up like the quills of a porcupine. If that was my master, he had a mask on his face. If that was my master, why did he cry out like a rat and run away?"

"It's all very odd," said Mr Utterson, "but I think I begin to understand. Your master must be afflicted with an illness that deforms the sufferer. The change of voice, the wearing of a mask, the way he avoids his friends, his desperation to find this drug ... He's looking for a cure. That's my explanation."

"Sir," said the butler, "do you think I don't know my master after twenty years? The thing in there is not Dr Jekyll. And it's my belief that murder has been done."

"Poole," replied Mr Utterson, "if you say that, then it's my duty to break in that door."

"Now you're talking!" cried the butler.

"Who is going to do it?" asked Utterson.

"You and me!" replied the butler, unafraid.

"Well," Mr Utterson smiled weakly. "I shall take full responsibility. Whatever happens, you will not be blamed."

"I'll use the axe," Poole said. "You can have the kitchen poker."

The lawyer took it and weighed it in his hand. "We are about to put ourselves in peril," he said. "Let us be frank with each other. We are both thinking more than we have said. This thing you saw ... did you recognise it?"

"Well, sir, it went so fast and the creature was so doubled up that I could hardly swear to that," said Poole. "But if you're asking if it was Mr Hyde, then yes, I think it was. Who else could have got in through that door? And it was the right size, had the same way of moving. And there was that odd feeling coming off him that makes your bone marrow turn cold and thin. Oh, I know it's not evidence, Mr Utterson, but I swear it was Mr Hyde!"

"I believe you," said the lawyer. "I believe poor Henry is dead. I believe his murderer still lurks in his room. We must be his avengers."

Utterson then told Poole to call the footman, who arrived in the kitchen looking pale with fear.

"Pull yourself together," said the lawyer. "I know this has been hard on you all, but now we're going to end it. Poole and I are going to force our way into the study. You and one of the other men must go around the corner. Carry large sticks. If anyone tries to escape out the back, stop them. We'll give you ten minutes to get in place."

As the footman left, Utterson looked at his watch. And then he tucked the poker under his arm and led the way into the yard.

Clouds covered the moon. The wind came in puffs that blew the candlelight to and fro as Utterson and Poole made their way into the theatre. The stillness was only broken by the sound of footsteps moving back and forwards overhead.

"It walks like that all day, sir," whispered Poole. "And most of the night. Only breaks off when a new sample arrives from a chemist. Listen, sir, and tell me – is that how my master walks?"

Poole was right. The steps were light and very different from the heavy, creaking tread of Henry Jekyll.

"Does it ever do anything else?" asked Utterson.

"Once I heard it weeping," said Poole. "Weeping like a woman, or a lost soul."

Ten minutes had passed. Poole picked up the axe. Both men crept towards the door.

"Jekyll," cried Utterson, "I demand to see you."

The footsteps stopped. But there was no reply.

"I must and will see you," cried Utterson again. "If not by your consent, then by force."

"Utterson," came the plea from behind the door. "For God's sake, have mercy."

"That's Hyde's voice!" yelled Utterson. "Down with the door, Poole!"

Poole swung the axe. The blow shook the building, and the red baize door leapt against its lock and hinges. A screech of animal terror rang from the study. The axe was swung again, and again the panels crashed and the frame shook. Four times the axe fell, but the wood was tough and the fittings well made. It was not until the fifth that the lock burst and the door fell inwards.

Utterson and Poole peered in, shaken by the terrible noise and the stillness that followed.

There in the lamplight, a fire glowed in the grate. A kettle hummed on it, and close by tea things were laid out. It would have been the most ordinary sight in London but for the glass-fronted cabinets full of chemicals.

Right in the middle of the room lay a man, his body contorted. They edged towards it and turned it on its back.

It was Edward Hyde, dressed in clothes far too big for him, clothes that were the doctor's size. The muscles of his face still twitched, but life was gone. The crushed test tube in his hand and the strong chemical smell hanging on the air told Utterson that Hyde had poisoned himself.

"We are too late," Utterson said gravely. "We cannot save Jekyll or punish Hyde. All we can do now is find your master's body."

The two men searched the building. They looked into every nook and cranny where a body might be hidden, but there was no trace of Henry Jekyll.

They returned to the study to begin another search. This time they examined the table. Heaps of white salt had been laid on glass saucers as if for an experiment. They looked at the full-length mirror, which had been tilted up to face the ceiling.

Mr Utterson said suddenly, "Why on earth would Jekyll want a mirror in his study?"

Poole didn't know. So they turned their attention to the desk. On top of a neat pile of papers was a large envelope addressed to Utterson in the doctor's handwriting. When the lawyer opened it, three smaller envelopes fell out.

The first was a copy of Henry Jekyll's will. It was the same as the one Utterson had in his safe, except that the name of Edward Hyde had been crossed out and replaced with that of Gabriel John Utterson.

Utterson stared at Poole, amazed. He looked at the will again and then at Hyde lying dead on the carpet.

"I don't understand!" Utterson exclaimed. "Hyde must have seen this! He would have been enraged. Why didn't he destroy this will?"

He picked up the second envelope. It was a brief note in the doctor's handwriting and dated that very same day.

"Poole!" the lawyer cried. "Jekyll was alive and here this very morning. He can't have been killed a week ago! He must still be alive – he must have fled! Why? How? And if he has ..." He looked at Hyde's body. "Was that really suicide? We must be careful. We might involve your master in some terrible catastrophe ..."

"Why don't you read the note, sir?" asked Poole.

"Because I'm afraid," replied Utterson. But he took a deep breath and read:

My dear Utterson,

By the time you read this, I will have disappeared. I cannot foresee what will happen, but instinct tells me the end is coming. Go and read the letter that Lanyon warned me he was going to place into your hands. And if you care to know more, read the confession of your unworthy and unhappy friend, Henry Jekyll.

"Was there a third envelope?" asked Utterson.

"Here, sir," said Poole, giving it to him.

Utterson put it straight into his pocket.

"Say nothing of this, Poole," he said. "If your master has fled or is dead, we may still be able to save his good name. It is now ten o'clock. I will go home and read what I need to, but I shall be back before midnight. Then we shall send for the police."

The two men went out, locking the door of the laboratory building behind them. Utterson left the servants still gathered about the fire in Jekyll's hall. He trudged back to his house to read the two narratives that would explain the whole mystery.

9
DR LANYON'S NARRATIVE

Four days ago, I received a letter from Henry Jekyll. I was surprised. I had dined with him only the night before, and we were not in the habit of writing to each other. The letter said:

Dear Lanyon,

We may have differed on scientific questions, but you are one of my oldest friends. If you ever said to me, "Jekyll, my life, my honour, my sanity depend on you," I would sacrifice my left hand to help you.

Lanyon, my life, my honour, my sanity now depend on you. If you fail me tonight, I am lost.

Cancel any plans. Come to my house. Poole, my butler, has his orders. He will be waiting with a locksmith. The door of my study must be forced open. You must go to the glass-fronted cabinet on the left-hand side and take out the drawer that is fourth from the top together with all its contents. Take it back to your house exactly as it is. If you set out now, you should be home before midnight.

At midnight, I ask you to be alone in your consulting room. A man will come to your house on my behalf. Open the front door and let him in yourself – do not let the servants see him. Give that man the drawer from my study. Once you have done that, you will have played your part and earned my eternal gratitude. Five minutes later, if you insist on an explanation, you will understand the vital importance of all this. If you do not do as I ask, I will die or lose my mind completely. If you do, all my troubles will roll away.

I am in a strange, dark place and very distressed, but you can help.

Save me, my dear Lanyon.
Your friend,
HJ

Henry Jekyll was clearly insane, but I felt I had to do as he asked. So I got into a cab and went straight to his house. I did exactly as he wished. When I returned home, I examined the contents of the drawer. There were packets of powders, neatly made up but not with the skill of a dispensing chemist. I presumed they'd been made by Jekyll. I opened one and found it contained a white, crystalline salt. There was also a test tube, half full of strong-smelling blood-red liquid. It seemed to contain phosphorus and some volatile ether. I could not guess the other ingredients.

There was a notebook that contained a series of dates covering a period of many years but stopping suddenly about twelve months ago. Here and there, a word or two was attached to a date – "double" occurred perhaps six times. Once, early on in the list, it stated: "Total failure!!!"

It all whetted my curiosity. How could these things affect the honour, sanity or life of my flighty friend? Why was I to pass this drawer on to a man sent by Jekyll? The more I thought, the more certain I was that Jekyll's mind was diseased. The whole thing troubled me. I sent my servants to bed, but I loaded my old revolver so that I could at least defend myself.

At midnight, there was a knock on the front door. I opened it and found a small man crouching against the pillars.

"Have you come from Dr Jekyll?" I asked.

He nodded, so I told him to come in. He did, casting a look behind at a policeman who was not far off. I kept my hand on my gun as I took him into my consulting room where I could see him clearly.

There was something very odd about the way I felt in his presence. He was dressed in clothes that were far too large for him. On an ordinary person, they might have looked comical, but there was something abnormal in the essence of this creature – something revolting.

"Have you got it?" he demanded. He laid a hand on my arm and shook me, sending an icy pang through my blood.

"Come, sir," I said as calmly as I could. "Be seated." I sat down myself and tried to behave as I would to any ordinary person.

The man was fighting rising panic. "I understood a drawer ..." he said.

When I pointed it out, he sprang at the thing with his teeth grating and his face so ghastly I feared for his life and sanity. At the sight of the contents, he uttered a loud sob of such immense relief that I sat petrified.

He asked for a measuring glass, and when I supplied it, he poured in a little of the blood-red liquid and added one of the powders. The mixture began to lighten in colour and effervesce. Small fumes of vapour rose, and the compound changed to dark purple and then watery green. He smiled and turned to look at me.

"Now," he said, "will you be wise? Will you let me leave with this glass in my hand without asking any questions? Or is your curiosity too greedy? Think before you answer. I can leave you as you were before. Or I can open a new realm of knowledge and new avenues to fame and power right here and now."

"Sir," said I, "I have gone too far with this not to see the end of it."

"Very well," replied my visitor. "But, Lanyon, remember the vows you made as a doctor. This is under the seal of our profession. You must not breathe a word to a living soul. You have been bound to the most narrow and material views, have mocked the virtue of transcendental medicine and have ridiculed your superiors – but now, behold!"

He put the glass to his lips and drank in one gulp. A cry followed. He reeled, staggered and clutched at the table, staring, gasping. As I looked, there came a change – he seemed to swell, his face seemed to melt and alter. I sprang to my feet and leapt back against the wall, my arm raised to shield me, my mind sunk with terror.

"Oh God! Oh God!" I screamed again and again. There before my eyes stood Henry Jekyll, pale and shaken and half fainting, groping before him with his hands like a man restored from death.

I cannot bring myself to write down what he told me in the next hour. I saw what I saw, I heard what I heard, and my soul sickened at it. Yet now when I ask myself if I believe it, I cannot answer. My life is shaken to its roots, sleep has left me, deadly terror sits beside me at all hours of the day and night. My days are numbered. I must die. I shall die incredulous. I cannot think of the wickedness that man revealed without a start of horror. I will say only one thing, Utterson, and that will be more than enough. The creature who crept into my house that night was known by the name of Hyde, on Jekyll's own confession. It was hunted in every corner of the land as the murderer of Sir Danvers Carew.

10

HENRY JEKYLL'S FULL STATEMENT OF THE CASE

I was born to a large fortune. Blessed with health and intelligence, I also had a fondness for hard work. I earned the respect of the wise and good among my fellow men and had a bright future ahead of me. My one fault was a tendency to high spirits, which conflicted with my desire to appear serious and worthy before the public. So I concealed my pleasures and excesses, and as a young man already led something of a double life. Yet I was no hypocrite. I did not pretend to be what I was not. When I was drunken and debauched, I was my true self. When I was doing good works amongst the poor and needy, I was also my true self. Both sides of me were equally sincere.

My scientific studies led me towards the mystic and transcendental. Little by little, I grew closer to the truth: that a man is not truly one single nature, but two. I began to daydream about separating the two elements. If each side of me could have a different identity, it would be such a relief! The bad twin could follow his own path to Hell and be unburdened by the remorse of his good twin. The good twin could walk the upward path to Heaven, no longer fearing he would be disgraced by his other half. But how could I split one from the other?

My laboratory provided the answer. I discovered certain chemicals that shook and pulled and re-shaped the body's flesh. I will not go into details here but say only that I managed to create a drug that could separate the good twin from the bad and set both free.

It was a long time before I put my theory to the test. I knew that I risked death by doing so, but at last the temptation overcame even that fear. I purchased a large quantity of a particular salt from a wholesale chemist, which was the last ingredient required. Late one night, I mixed the elements, watched them boil and smoke, and drank the potion.

At once, I was racked with pain: a grinding of bones, a deadly nausea, a horror of the spirit. But when the agonies faded, there was something wonderful and new and sweet in every sensation. I felt younger, lighter, happier in my body. An intense recklessness, a current of sensual images streamed into my mind. As I took my first breath in this new body, I knew myself to be evil, and the knowledge of this strengthened and delighted me like drinking fine wine. I stretched out my hands and was suddenly aware that I was smaller.

There was no mirror in my study then. The one there now was brought in later so I could watch my transformations. That night, I crept like a thief along the corridors of my own house. In my dressing room, I saw Edward Hyde for the first time.

He was much smaller, slighter and younger than Henry Jekyll. He repulsed everyone he met. Yet that night, I felt a leap of welcome when I looked at that small, ugly figure in the mirror. This, too, was myself. A livelier, brighter form than the divided self I was so used to seeing.

I lingered only a moment before the mirror. The second part of my experiment was yet to come. I had to hurry back to my study and prepare and drink another cup of potion. Then I would feel the pains of dissolving and return to the face and character and form of Henry Jekyll.

I must say here that I believe the reason Hyde was smaller than Jekyll is that the evil side of my nature was less robust and well developed than the good. After all, most of life is nine tenths effort and self-control. We are born selfish and are taught to be good and kind and generous. We have to exercise that side of ourselves every day as we grow.

As for the reason people had an instinctive aversion to Hyde? That is easy to explain. Every human being is a mixture of good and bad elements. But I had separated them, so Edward Hyde was pure, distilled evil.

Let me also say that the drug was neither diabolical nor divine: it simply shook the doors of the prison-house of my disposition. The drug did not decide what I would become: I did. Everything would have been different if I had conducted my experiment in a noble, generous spirit. I could have emerged from the agonies of death and birth as an angel, not a devil.

From that day on, I had two characters and two appearances. One was pure evil, as I have said. But the other was the same old Henry Jekyll, who had not been improved or reformed in any way. He was still inclined to high spirits and indulging in shameful pleasures. As I was getting older, these tendencies put my reputation at greater risk and had become increasingly unwelcome. But now my new power opened a world of opportunities!

I only had to drink the potion to shed Jekyll's body and wrap myself in Hyde's as if it were a thick cloak. Then I could do whatever I desired. It all seemed so funny! As Edward Hyde, I took and furnished the house in Soho. As Henry Jekyll, I told my servants that Mr Hyde was to have the freedom of my house in the square. I drew up a will so that if anything befell Dr Jekyll, I could continue to live as Edward Hyde.

Fully prepared, I began to exploit the strange immunity of my position. Men have often hired thugs to do their crimes. I was the first that ever did so to commit pleasures. Dr Jekyll could plod along respectably in public and then, in a moment of temptation, strip off his identity like a schoolboy and spring into a sea of liberty. I was perfectly safe. I did not even exist! I could slip into my laboratory, swallow the potion, and Edward Hyde melted away like breath on a mirror, no matter what he had done. And there in his place, sitting quietly at home, was Dr Jekyll.

The pleasures I first sought were undignified, that is all. But they soon became monstrous. Hyde was evil. Villainous. Everything centred on himself.

He drank pleasure from torturing others. He was relentless, like a man of stone. Henry Jekyll was aghast at the crimes of Edward Hyde and shocked at his depravity. But Jekyll reasoned that it was Hyde, and Hyde alone, that was guilty! So my virtue slept while my vice stayed awake and was alert to every opportunity.

And then an act of cruelty to a child drew the anger of your friend, Mr Enfield. I had to write that cheque and sign it in my own name. I had drawn attention to myself. After that, I opened an account at another bank in the name of Hyde. I sloped my handwriting backwards and gave my evil twin his own signature. I had solved the problem! I thought I was beyond the reach of fate – that this could all go on for ever.

But two months before the murder of Sir Danvers, I woke confused. I could see I was at home in the house in the square, yet something whispered that I was in the room in Soho where I slept as Edward Hyde. I lay in bed, dropping in and out of sleep until I noticed my hand.

The hand of Henry Jekyll was large, white, firm and clean. The hand I saw was lean, dirty and hairy. It was the hand of Edward Hyde.

I must have stared at it for half a minute before terror woke me like a cymbal crash. Leaping from my bed, I rushed to the mirror. My blood seemed to grow thin and icy. I had gone to bed as Henry Jekyll but woken as Edward Hyde. How was it to be explained? How was it to be remedied? It was morning. The servants were up. My drugs were all in the study. It was a while before I remembered that the servants were used to Hyde being about the place. They were surprised to see him at such an hour, but I passed through the house to my laboratory and the study, and ten minutes later Dr Jekyll returned.

The incident troubled me. I began to see that the balance of my two halves might be overthrown. The power of changing from one to the other might fail. I might become Edward Hyde permanently. I knew the drug was not always reliable. Once, early in my career, it had totally failed. Since then, I had doubled the amount and sometimes even trebled it. In the beginning, it had been hard to throw off the body of Henry Jekyll, but the power had shifted to the other side. I was losing my better self. The worse was taking me over.

I had to choose between the two. My two natures shared one memory, but nothing else.

As I have said, Jekyll contained both: he shared in the adventures of Hyde – sometimes with fear, sometimes with greedy gusto. Hyde was purely evil and utterly indifferent to Jekyll. To him, the doctor was only a place to hide from pursuit. If I became only Jekyll, the excesses I indulged in would have to end. If I became only Hyde, everything fine and noble would vanish, and I would be despised and friendless. But Jekyll would suffer in the fire of abstinence. Hyde would not even notice what he had lost.

I did what most would do. I said farewell to the liberty, youth and secret pleasures I had enjoyed in the disguise of Hyde. Once more, I became only the doctor, surrounded by his friends. I chose the better part of myself but then found I hadn't the strength to stick to it. I neither gave up the house in Soho nor destroyed Hyde's clothes.

For two months, I led a good life, until I began to be tortured with wicked longings. In a moment of weakness, I made and swallowed the transforming drug to become Hyde again.

My devil had been caged for two months: Hyde came out roaring. The spirit of hell had awoken in me, and it raged. With wild glee, I struck Sir Danvers like a sick child breaks a plaything. I tasted delight in every blow. And then I fled the scene for the house in Soho. I destroyed my papers, then went through the streets gloating on my crime. I devised other evil deeds while I listened for the sounds of pursuit. Hyde had a song on his lips as he made up another dose of the drug. He toasted his victim as he drank. The pangs of transformation still tore at him as Henry Jekyll fell on his knees, lifted clasped hands to God and prayed with streaming tears of remorse running down his face.

I resolved in future to redeem the past. I laboured hard to relieve others' suffering. I did good works, and I enjoyed it. But the lower side of me began to growl almost at once. Yet I did not mix the potion; I did not bring back Hyde. It was as an ordinary, secret sinner that I fell once more into temptation. And that was what finally destroyed the balance of my soul.

It was a fine, clear January day, wet underfoot where the frost had melted, but cloudless overhead. Regent's Park was full of birdsong and sweet with the smell of spring. I sat on a bench in the sun, the animal within me licking the chops of memory. My spiritual side faded, promising penitence at some future point but not quite now. *After all, I am just like other men*, I thought. And then I smiled, remembering all my good deeds. *No, I told myself, I am better than most!*

The moment that vain thought came into my head, I was seized with nausea and deadly shuddering. The spasm passed, leaving me faint. And then everything changed. I felt suddenly bold. I despised danger. My clothes hung limp and baggy on my shrunken limbs. My hands were lean and hairy. I was Edward Hyde. A moment before, I had been a wealthy, respected, beloved citizen. Now I was a hunted, homeless, known murderer, headed for the gallows.

My sanity wavered but did not fail. As Hyde, my senses were sharpened to a fine point. My drugs were in my study. How would I reach them?

In the end, I thought of Lanyon and remembered that my handwriting was still my own. I arranged my over-large clothes as best I could and took a cab to an inn where I rented a room. His life in danger, Hyde was a creature shaken with anger, strung to the pitch of murder, lusting to inflict pain. Yet he was also intelligent. He wrote to Lanyon and to Poole, issuing instructions. And then nothing lived in him but fear and hatred until night came and he made his way to Lanyon's house in Cavendish Square.

I drank the potion at Lanyon's and came to myself, and the horror in my old friend's eyes perhaps affected me. I don't know. It was a drop in the ocean. I was no longer gripped by a fear of the gallows. I feared becoming Hyde again. I was partly in a dream as I talked to Lanyon. I was still in a dream when I came home and got into bed. I awoke shaken – weak yet also refreshed. I hated and feared the brute that slept within me, but I was at home and close to my drugs. Gratitude for my escape shone almost as brightly as hope.

I was walking across the yard, drinking in the chill air, when I felt the change once more coming on me. It took a double dose of the drugs to recall me to myself. Six hours later, the pangs returned, and I had to take more. From that day on, I was only able to wear the appearance of Jekyll after taking the drug. If I slept – if I dozed even for a moment in my chair – I woke as Hyde. I condemned myself to sleeplessness. I became a creature emptied by fever, weak in body and mind, consumed with the horror of my other self.

Hyde's mind brimmed with images of terror. His soul boiled with pointless hatred. His body could not contain the raging energy within. But the powers of Hyde had grown as Jekyll sickened. The hate that divided them was equal on both sides. To Jekyll, Hyde was a slimy thing that had crawled from the mud and yet was closer to him than a wife. Hyde was caged in Jekyll's flesh, always struggling to be born.

Hyde's hatred for Jekyll was different. Fear of the gallows forced him to hide, but he hated it. He hated Jekyll's weakness, hated that Jekyll disliked him, feared Jekyll would murder him by suicide.

It might have gone on for years, but the salt I needed for the potion began to run low. I sent out for a fresh supply, but it was not the same. You will know from Poole that I have ransacked the chemists of London. I am sure now that the first batch all those years ago was impure, and it was that unknown impurity that made the potion work.

A week has passed since then. I am finishing this under the influence of the very last of the old salt. This is the last time that Henry Jekyll can think his own thoughts, see his own face in the mirror. Half an hour from now, I will forever be Hyde again. Will he die upon the scaffold? Or will he have the courage to release himself by his own hand before then? God knows. This is my true hour of death. It is here that I lay down the pen and proceed to seal up my confession. And in doing so, I bring the life of that unhappy Henry Jekyll to an end.

Our books are tested
for children and young people by
children and young people.

Thanks to everyone who consulted on
a manuscript for their time and effort in
helping us to make our books better
for our readers.